VLAD

– AND THE –
GREAT FIRE OF LONDON

WRITTEN BY KATE CUNNINGHAM

ILLUSTRATED BY SAM CUNNINGHAM

In fact Boxton is more than a friend.

You could call him my friendly home from home.

This is where I live, on the fur between Boxton's ears.

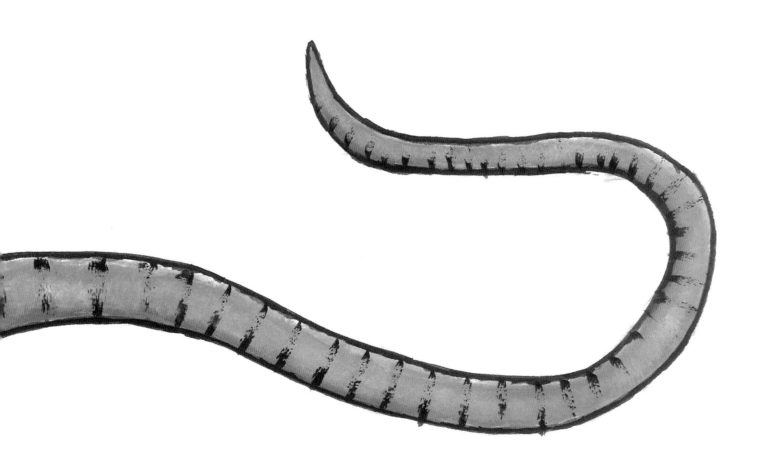

Boxton is great. He knows where the tastiest rubbish is and where I can get a little snack of blood off a delicious human.

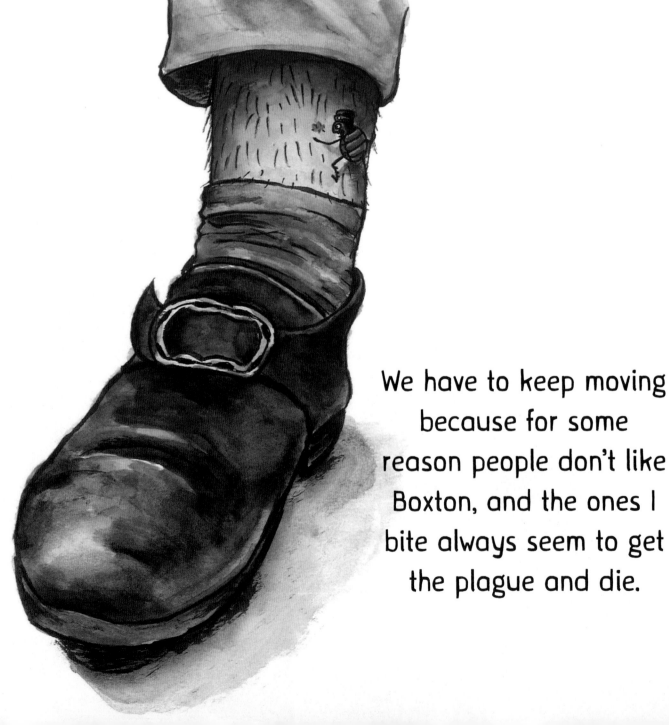

We have to keep moving because for some reason people don't like Boxton, and the ones I bite always seem to get the plague and die.

Everything was wonderful until three days ago.

We were full up so we lay down to sleep.
The night was warm and cosy;
it was almost hot for September.

SMOKE!

I leapt up and started hopping around on Boxton's head. He was dozy and did not want to move, but I bit him hard. That woke him up!

The flames were burning brightly in the huge
wood pile that the baker used for his oven.
The fire was blazing up the wall and was
now moving across the floor towards us.

We had to move quickly. I held on tightly to Boxton's
hair as he squeezed through a gap in the door.

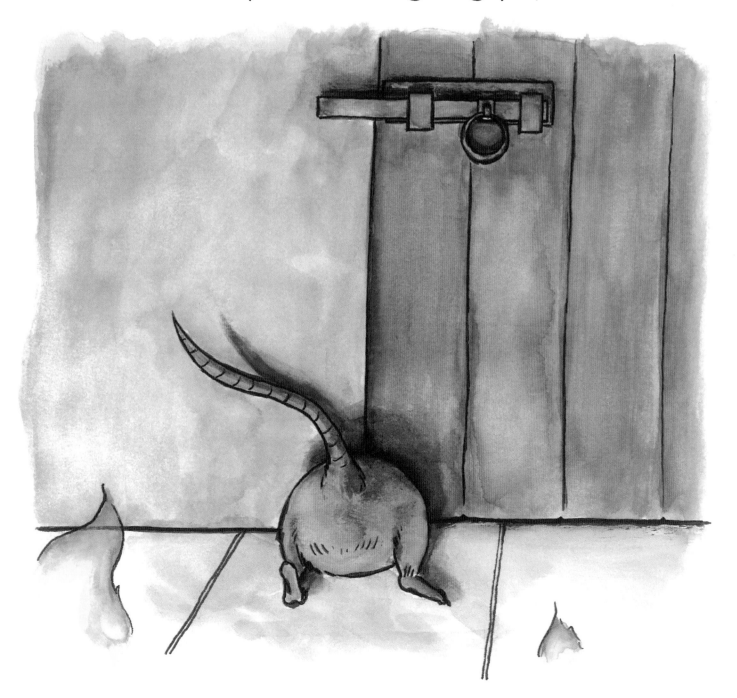

We were free, but the fire had spread to other houses.

All around us people were running and
screaming. Some were carrying crying children,
or pulling carts piled high with furniture.

If we stayed here we would get burnt,
but if we moved we might be squashed
by hooves, or feet, or wheels.

We ran (well Boxton ran,
I shouted encouragement).

He scampered along the cobbles, slipping through the mud and leaping over puddles of smelly water and around piles of horse poo. I clung to his sweaty back, terrified that I'd slip off.

Finally, we came to the edge of the River Thames.

Boxton stopped, panting loudly.

Suddenly there was a
massive explosion.

We looked back and we could see soldiers blowing up people's homes. Buildings were collapsing and now there was a gap between the burning houses and the ones that could be saved. But still the fire burned the wooden walls and thatched roofs.

The wind blew, fanning the inferno and the flames went from red to white. Smoke filled the air making the sky dark and the falling ash scorched our tongues and made us choke.

Sparks were flying around and some landed on Boxton's tail and singed his fur. He squeaked and jumped and ran once more past London Bridge.

The bridge was full of people and soldiers, so we turned and headed towards the Tower of London. Boxton's nose was quivering. I could only smell burning wood, but I knew that my friend had sniffed something else.

On he staggered until we came to a garden.

In the middle of a patch of soil knelt a scared, chubby man in a long coat and wig. He was digging a hole and talking to himself.

"It will be safe there, Samuel." he was muttering.

He put his precious possessions into the hole,
some bottles and a small, stinky parcel.

Looking around he checked that no one was
watching before he covered it and hurried away.

Boxton crept closer to where the bundle had been on the ground. There, where it had leaked, lay crumbs of cheese! Boxton bent down and gobbled each piece before sighing and lying down to rest.

Slowly we turned to follow the crowds trudging along the road.

Ahead of us were fields. People put down their belongings and started to make shelters out of blankets.

It looked like we would be camping here for some time as in the distance the fire continued to rage.

FACT FILE

The Great Fire of London burned for 3 days from 2nd September 1666.

It started around 1 o'clock in the morning, in the bakery
of Thomas Farriner on Pudding Lane.

There was no Fire Brigade so people had to work together carrying
water and pulling down buildings to stop the fire. After the fire, private
fire brigades were started, but it was another 167 years (not until 1833)
that there was one organised fire service across London.

Samuel Pepys lived in Seething Lane near the Tower of London.
He wrote in his diary that he buried his wine and his parmesan
cheese to save it from the fire. The fire was put out before it
reached his house.

Nobody knows exactly how many people died in the fire.
Officially there were six deaths (including the baker's maid)
but many poor people probably did not get recorded.

Thousands of London refugees left with whatever they could carry.
They set up camps in the fields around London.

This is how big Vlad really is

For Sue who gave us a love of books
and suggested we make this book together.

With thanks to everyone who supported us in this venture,
especially Sean, Danny and Freddie.
Any errors are the responsibility of the author.

VLAD AND THE GREAT FIRE OF LONDON

Written by Kate Cunningham
Illustrated by Sam Cunningham

This paperback edition published 2016 by Reading Riddle

This edition designed by Rachel Lawston, lawstondesign.com

www.readingriddle.co.uk

ISBN: 978-0-9955205-0-9